MONKEY FOR SALE

SANNA STANLEY

Frances Foster Books • Farrar, Straus and Giroux • New York

Luzolo had a five-franc coin to spend at market.

"Don't buy the first thing you see," said her father. "Look around, choose what you really want, and then bargain for a fair price."

"And remember, Luzolo," added her mother, "no one gets something for nothing on market day."

Most of the time, the people in Luzolo's village bartered and traded goods and services, but once a month it was market day. On market day people came from the surrounding villages and even from the city to buy and sell.

"Beans! Rice! Combs and candy!" At every stall people called out, loudly advertising their goods. Luzolo walked by stands piled high with manioc and spicy hot peppers. She walked by fabric and clay pots, baskets and T-shirts.

She saw a bag of mango candy and almost bought it, but remembered what her father had said, and walked on.

Then Luzolo saw a display of shiny bottles of fingernail polish.
She reached out to touch a bright red one.

"That color would look nice on you," said the salesman.

"It's my favorite color," said Luzolo, holding it up. "How much?" she asked.

"Five francs," said the salesman.

Luzolo remembered that her father had told her to bargain.

"Three francs," she offered.

"Not enough," said the man. "Four."

"Okay," said Luzolo, and handed the man her coin.

He gave her a one-franc coin in return.

On into the market a woman was roasting peanuts and frying mukatis, Luzolo's favorite fried-dough treat.

The smell made Luzolo hungry.

"How much for one packet of peanuts and one packet of mukatis?" Luzolo asked.

"Two francs," said the woman.

"One," Luzolo said firmly, and held out her coin.

"Done," said the woman. She rolled two pieces of newspaper into cones and filled one with peanuts, the other with mukatis.

"Time for a snack," Luzolo said to an interested village dog.

The dog barked for his snack while Luzolo looked around and found a place to sit.

"No one gets something for nothing on market day," Luzolo told the dog. "Do a trick."

She held out a mukati. The dog stood on his hind legs and begged. He was rewarded with some fresh, warm mukatis.

Luzolo's best friend, Kiese, came running through the market.

"Luzolo, look what I got!" Kiese called. She held out a fistful of colored plastic strands that the village girls liked to weave into bracelets.

"And look what I have!" Luzolo exclaimed, showing Kiese the bottle of red fingernail polish.

"I'll trade you . . ." the girls said at the same time.

They wove the plastic strands into bracelets, and then painted each other's fingernails with the shiny red polish. All around them, people were shouting, talking, and bargaining.

"Manioc! Peanuts! Beans! Rice! Tin cups! . . . Monkey for sale!"

"Did someone say 'monkey for sale'?" asked Luzolo.

"It sounds like Mama Lusufu," said Kiese. "And if she has a monkey . . ."

"We better hurry!" Luzolo cried, and they took off running. Both girls knew that Mama Lusufu would sell anything she could get her hands on, even a jungle animal.

Sure enough, a monkey was tied to Mama Lusufu's stall.

"Would he make a good pet?" asked a man from the city.

"The best pet ever," said Mama Lusufu, "and he's yours for fifteen francs."

"Ridiculous," said the man. "No more than ten . . ."

"Fourteen." Mama Lusufu lowered her price.

"Ten," insisted the man.

"Ridiculous!" shouted Mama Lusufu.

"We'll see," said the man. "I'll be back."

"Mama Lusufu, you can't sell a monkey!" Luzolo cried out.

"I caught him, and I will sell him," said Mama Lusufu.

"*Please* give us the monkey," Luzolo pleaded.

"We'll trade you everything we have," Kiese said.

"No, girls. I am selling this monkey to buy a new water pot. Mine broke when I was chasing this rascal out of my garden," said Mama Lusufu. "After he ate my food!" she added.

"Water pot?" Kiese asked, and she nudged Luzolo. Kiese's mother made the water pots for the village.

"If we get you a water pot, will you give us the monkey?" Luzolo asked Mama Lusufu.

"*If* I still have the monkey and you get me a nice water pot, we'll make a deal," said Mama Lusufu. "But a good water pot is very expensive . . ."

Kiese's mother was completing a sale.

She smiled when Kiese said that Mama Lusufu wanted a water pot.

"What a lucky day," said Kiese's mother. "If Mama Lusufu buys a water pot from me, I can buy an embroidery from Luzolo's mother. Your mother does the best embroidery in the village," she said to Luzolo.

The girls headed for Luzolo's mother's stall.

"Mama, Mama," Luzolo cried, "Kiese's mother wants an embroidery."

"Good," said Luzolo's mother. "Then I can buy some new tin cups."

"No!" Luzolo cried.

"No?" her father asked, and pointed to Luzolo's bright red fingernails. "You got what you wanted, shouldn't your mama get what she wants?"

"No, what I *really* want is the monkey!" Luzolo cried.

"Monkey!" said both her parents at the same time.

The girls explained that Mama Lusufu was selling the monkey to buy a water pot from Kiese's mother who wanted an embroidery . . .

"And Mama wants tin cups," Luzolo's father added. "But what do you think the tin cup salesman wants?"

When Luzolo and Kiese found the tin cup salesman, he pointed to a woman selling baskets. "What I want is one of those handwoven baskets for my wife," he told the girls. They hurried on to see the basket weaver.

"Please," Luzolo said to the basket weaver, "we need a very nice basket."

"How much will you give me?" asked the woman.

"Everything we have," said Kiese.

"That's really nice stuff," said the woman, glancing at the nail polish and the bracelets. "But what I need is beans and rice."

"Beans and rice!" said Luzolo. "Everyone has beans and rice!"

"Almost everyone," said the woman with a smile.

The basket weaver was right. Almost every villager had little piles of beans and rice for sale. It was no problem at all to trade two bracelets and an almost full bottle of red fingernail polish for several small packets of beans and rice.

The basket weaver was delighted with the packets of beans and rice and, in exchange, gave the girls the very nice basket she had just finished.

The tin cup salesman said his wife would love the basket, and he handed over four blue tin cups with flowers painted on them.

Luzolo's mother said the cups were exactly the ones she wanted, and she gave the girls her very best embroidery to take to Kiese's mother.

Kiese's mother said the embroidery was perfect, and she picked out a big, beautiful water pot for Mama Lusufu.

"Go carefully, and slowly," said Kiese's mother, placing the pot on Kiese's head.

The man from the city was back, bargaining for the monkey at Mama Lusufu's stall. "Ten francs," he said firmly.

"Twelve," Mama Lusufu shouted.

"Eleven," said the man, holding out his change.

"Mama Lusufu!" Luzolo interrupted.

"You said if we got you a water pot you would give *us* the monkey!" Kiese cried out.

"I said if I still had the monkey," said Mama Lusufu, "and I'm selling him right now."

She turned to glare at the girls, and the water pot caught her attention.

"That is a very nice water pot," said Mama Lusufu, and she reached for the pot on Kiese's head. "Very nice," she said again.

"I'm sorry, but monkeys don't make such good pets," she told the man from the city. "They eat too much.

"A deal is a deal," she said to the girls.

Mama Lusufu handed the
monkey's rope to Luzolo.

The monkey stretched and
reached for it.

"Oh, no, you won't be needing
that where we're taking you . . ."
Luzolo told the monkey.

"See, you're going home," said
Kiese.

The monkey jumped into
Luzolo's arms with a squeal, and
the girls headed for the edge of
the jungle.

When Kiese untied the rope, the
monkey jumped out of Luzolo's
arms, scampered away, and climbed
up into the trees.

"Next time, stay away from
Mama Lusufu!" Luzolo called
to the monkey.

But he wasn't listening.

For Paul

The art for this book was made using two printmaking
processes: etching and hand-painted *Chine collé* on
mulberry paper.

Distributed in Canada by Douglas & McIntyre Ltd.
Color separations by Hong Kong Scanner Arts
Printed and bound in the United States by Berryville Graphics
Designed by Nancy Goldenberg
First edition, 2002
1 3 5 7 9 10 8 6 4 2

Library of Congress Cataloging-in-Publication Data
Stanley, Sanna.
    Monkey for sale / Sanna Stanley.— 1st ed.
        p.   cm.
    Summary: When Luzolo goes to market with her parents, she
learns that it takes a great deal of bartering to finally get what
she wants.
    ISBN 0-374-35017-5
    [1. Markets—Fiction.   2. Barter—Fiction.   3. Congo (Democratic
Republic)—Fiction.]   I. Title.
PZ7.S7895 M1 2002
[E]—dc21
                                                        00-50389